WILD THINGS!

Lion
who came to lunch

Lisa Regan

ILLUSTRATED BY **Kelly Byrne**

BLOOMSBURY

LONDON BERLIN NEW YORK SYDNEY

Published 2011 by
Bloomsbury Publishing PLC
49–51 Bedford Square, London, WC1B 3DP

www.bloomsbury.com

ISBN   HB 978-1-4081-4244-8
           PB 978-1-4081-5681-0

This book is produced using paper that is made from wood grown in managed, sustainable forests. It is natural, renewable and recyclable. The logging and manufacturing processes conform to the environmental regulations of the country of origin.

Produced for Bloomsbury Publishing by Calcium. www.calciumcreative.co.uk

Illustrated by Kelly Bryne

Picture acknowledgements: Shutterstock: Chris Kruger 23tl, Graeme Shannon 23tr.

Printed in China by Toppan Leefung

All the internet addresses given in this book were correct at the time of going to press. The author and publishers regret any inconvenience caused if addresses have changed or sites have ceased to exist, but can accept no responsibility for any such changes.

County Council

Libraries, books and more . . .

	0 4 FEB 2012	
0 2 MAY 2013		
0 2 MAY 2013	1 9 SEP 2012	
31/8/18		
LOL 10/23		
	1 APR 2023	
	2 2 NOV 2024	

Please return/renew this item by the last due date.
Library items may be renewed by phone on
030 33 33 1234 (24 hours) or via our website

www.cumbria.gov.uk/libraries

Cumbria Libraries

Interactive Catalogue

Ask for a CLIC password

Contents

Ring, ring. Wild thing!

If you're WILD about animals, today's your lucky day.

There's a lion at the door! Are you brave enough to invite it in?

Grrr!

A lion will certainly scare away unwanted visitors...

5

Show off!

Male lions shake their **manes** to make them bigger.

A big mane frightens **enemies** and attracts lady lions.

You will need

hair mousse

hairspray (not really!)

oh dear

Adult lions have REALLY LONG claws.

They are as long as your fingers!

You will need

to train your lion to wear **mittens**

8

Boing!

Leaping lions! Look how well they can jump.

You will need

lots of space to play

Your friends may be too scared to join in, though...

Catch!

11

Tea time

Lions are mighty meat eaters.

They eat A LOT: the same as 240 burgers in one go.

You will need

meat

more meat

some more meat

12

Phewee!

All that meat can mean only one thing...

Stinky poos!
A meat-only diet
makes a really
bad smell.

You will need

a clothes peg for
your nose

Yuck!

BATHROOM

Better bring in
the **air fresheners**.

15

Shhh

Lions are famous
for their roar.

The mighty
lion call can be
heard miles away.

You will need

ear plugs

Time to go home

The lion seems happy, but your parents really aren't!

18

It's time to post your pet
back to its real home...

A cat makes a great pet,
but a lion is a WILD THING!

Cool creatures

Lions live in Africa and Asia. There are only about 300 Asian lions left – they live in a tiny part of India.

Asian lions eat **prey** such as deer, antelope, water buffalo and wild boar.

Only male lions have a mane. The mane of an Asian lion is short enough for you to see its ears.

A 'pride' of lions is a group that lives together. Asian prides are small and are made up of about two related females and their young. African lions live in larger prides.

When they're hunting, **lionesses** are in charge. They chase and kill prey, then the male lions join in the feast.

A lion has huge, sharp claws and teeth to catch its prey and bring it to the ground. They have no chewing teeth, so they swallow big lumps whole!

Glossary

air fresheners sprays that make a room smell good

enemies people or animals that might harm you

hair mousse a product for styling hair

hairspray a product for styling hair

lionesses female lions

manes the long, shaggy hair around a lion's head

mittens woolly gloves

poser someone who shows off

prey animals that are hunted for food

Thanks for having me!

The Zoological Society of London (ZSL) is a charity that provides help for animals at home and worldwide. We also run ZSL London Zoo and ZSL Whipsnade Zoo.

By buying this book, you have helped us raise money to continue our work with animals around the world.

Find out more at zsl.org

ZSL
LIVING CONSERVATION

ZSL
LONDON
ZOO

ZSL
WHIPSNADE
ZOO

Take them all home!

ISBN   HB 978-1-4081-4247-9
PB 978-1-4081-5678-0

ISBN   HB 978-1-4081-4246-2
PB 978-1-4081-5679-7

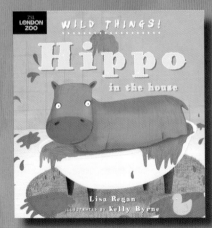

ISBN   HB 978-1-4081-4245-5
PB 978-1-4081-5680-3

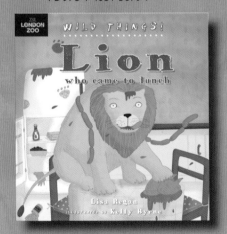

ISBN   HB 978-1-4081-4244-8
PB 978-1-4081-5681-0